The EASTER BEAR

Story by
John Barrett

Illustrations by
Rick Reinert Productions

Developed by
The LeFave Company

Ideals Publishing Corp.

ISBN 0-8249-8007-7

Ted Edward Bear peeked from beneath his warm blanket. He stretched and yawned. He looked at his alarm clock. "A quarter till Spring? I wish I could sleep another month!"

The young bear climbed out of bed and opened the front door. "Brrrrrr," he shivered as he picked up the morning paper. The bold, black headline read:

RABBITS GO ON STRIKE!

"Oh my," muttered Ted.

Ted sat at the breakfast table and read the newspaper:

> Members of the Rabbit Union—Egg Workers Local #139—went on strike today. All egg production, coloring and delivery has stopped. The union leader, Nick the Bunny, was quoted as saying, "Spring always comes after we deliver the Easter Eggs. With us rabbits on strike, there won't be any Spring this year."

On his way to the bus stop, Ted knocked at the door of his friend, Bum Bear. The elderly bear lived in an old house with a dirt floor.

"Good morning, Mr. Bear," said Ted. "Have you heard the terrible news?"

"What news?" asked Bum Bear.

"The rabbits are on strike," Ted announced. There won't be any Easter Eggs. And without the eggs, Spring won't come."

Bum Bear smiled. "Don't worry about Spring," he said softly. "It will be along directly."

Ted felt better. He knew his friend was a very wise bear.

Ted Edward Bear worked at the Bureau of Bear Affairs. The Bureau was full of departments and divisions that looked after things bears couldn't do anything about. "It is a perfect government agency," said C. Emory Bear, the head of the Bureau.

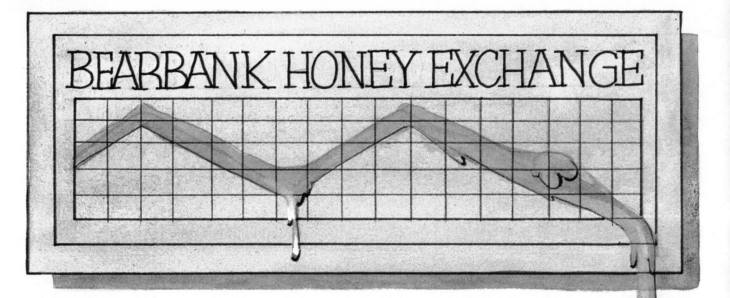

The other bears at the Bureau were worried. Without Spring, there wouldn't be any flowers. Without flowers, the bees couldn't make honey. And without honey, the City of Bearbank would have to shut down. Honey was the bears' main source of energy.

Ted Edward Bear walked straight to the chief executive's office. "I would like to talk to you about the rabbit strike," Ted said politely.

C. Emory Bear smiled. "That's what I like — a bear who tackles a problem with both paws!"

"I'm not sure it is a problem," Ted tried to explain. "You see, my friend Bum...."

"Of course it isn't a problem," the head of the Bureau interrupted. He looked at the young bear. "I like your attitude."

"I'd like to explain...." Ted stammered.

"Yes, of course," C. Emory interrupted. "Explain later. First we must go talk with those twitchy little rabbits!"

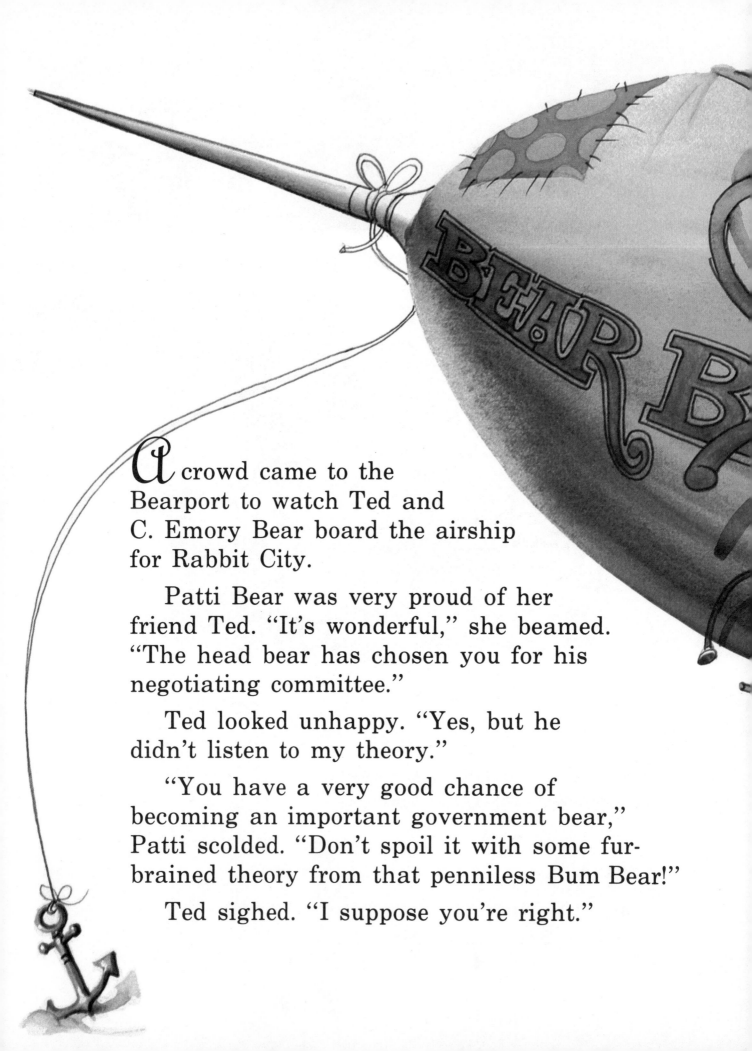

$\mathcal{A}$ crowd came to the Bearport to watch Ted and C. Emory Bear board the airship for Rabbit City.

Patti Bear was very proud of her friend Ted. "It's wonderful," she beamed. "The head bear has chosen you for his negotiating committee."

Ted looked unhappy. "Yes, but he didn't listen to my theory."

"You have a very good chance of becoming an important government bear," Patti scolded. "Don't spoil it with some fur-brained theory from that penniless Bum Bear!"

Ted sighed. "I suppose you're right."

$\mathcal{T}$ed and his boss, arrived at Rabbit City and went straight to the egg plant. All work had stopped.

The leader of the rabbit union, Nick the Bunny, pulled a list of demands from his furry pocket.

He read in a loud voice, "We rabbits
want the following: 1. Rabbits will get a
30% weekly wage increase. 2. The rabbit
will be called 'King of the Beasts'!"

$\mathcal{B}$earforce One returned to Bearbank. "It is outrageous," thundered C. Emory Bear. "A rabbit can't be 'King of the Beasts'!"

Reporters crowded around the chief executive. One asked, "But what about Spring?"

C. Emory Bear thought for a moment. "If the rabbits won't deliver the eggs, we bears will."

The television reporters then turned to Ted. "What do you think?" they asked.

"Well," said Ted, "Bum Bear says Spring will be along directly...without the eggs."

The bears looked at Ted and laughed.

At Grizzly University, the reporters interviewed Dr. Werner Von Bear. He was Bearbank's most respected professor. He said, "There is evidence the Earth has gone through several ice ages—times when there was no Spring or Summer. We have always wondered what caused these ice ages. Now we know. These were times in the Earth's history when the bunnies were on strike."

$\mathcal{C}$. Emory Bear ordered the bears into action. "This will be a crash program," he announced. "We bears will pitch in and save the world from an ice age."

They cooked eggs.

They painted eggs.

And they...

whooooops!

𝒯ed went to Bum Bear's house. "I've come to apologize," said Ted. "Everybody in Bearbank is laughing at us."

"It doesn't matter if other bears laugh," said Bum Bear. "Not as long as we are right."

Ted looked sad. "But they say Spring won't come."

The older bear smiled. "Come in."

Ted entered the humble home. It was warm inside. He looked down. The dirt floor had a beautiful carpet of flowers.

"I plant them every year," said the wise old bear.

"If the flowers are growing, then Spring is coming," Ted babbled excitedly.

"That's right," said Bum Bear. "You can go back and tell your friends there's nothing to worry about."

Ted dashed to the Bureau of Bear Affairs. The rabbits were now picketing the government office. They pointed at Ted and laughed. "There's the bear who says Spring will come without our eggs."

Patti Bear was tearful. "Everybody in Bearbank is laughing at you," she cried.

"But I have the solution," said Ted happily. "If I could just speak to the rabbits, I think we could settle the strike."

C. Emory Bear glanced at the picketing rabbits. "Hmmmmmph," he gruffed. "Maybe those fumblebunnies will listen to you. But don't start any more fur-brained foolishness."

"No, sir," said Ted with a smile.

Giggling bears and laughing rabbits gathered as Ted Edward Bear prepared to speak.

"Rabbits don't bring Spring," Ted said. "Neither do bears. Rabbits and bears bring gifts which warm the hearts of children all over the world. But it is the warmth of the sun that brings Spring."

The rabbits and the bears looked doubtful.

Ted pointed toward the rear of the crowd. "Spring is already here," he smiled.

The rabbits and the bears turned to look.

There stood Bum Bear with the biggest bouquet of Spring flowers they had ever seen!

"*I* guess the rabbit can't be 'King of the Beasts,'" muttered Nick the Bunny.

"Rabbits bring happiness to children," Ted said. "That's more than any king could ever do. You are better than kings!"

The bunnies smiled proudly.

"Better than kings...?" Nick the Bunny looked at the smiling rabbits. "In that case, we'll just forget about the strike and go back to work."

The rabbits, with years of experience, speed, and organization, pitched in to help the bears. Within hours, Easter Eggs were on the way to children all over the world.

The next morning, Ted Edward Bear found a big, beautiful Easter Egg on his doorstep.

And Spring came to Bearbank.